epic!

UNICORN ISLAND

Donna Galanti

Illustrated by Bethany Stancliffe

Andrews McMeel
PUBLISHING®

Andrews McMeel Publishing
a division of Andrews McMeel Universal
1130 Walnut Street, Kansas City, Missouri 64106

www.andrewsmcmeel.com

Epic Creations, Inc.
702 Marshall Street, Suite 280,
Redwood City, California 94063

www.getepic.com

21 22 23 24 25 SDB 10 9 8 7 6 5 4 3 2 1

ISBN: 978-1-5248-6470-5

Library of Congress Control Number: 2020941753

Design by Carolyn Bahar

Made by:
King Yip (Dongguan) Printing & Packaging Factory Ltd.
Address and location of manufacturer:
Daning Administrative District, Humen Town
Dongguan Guangdong, China 523930
1st Printing – 11/2/20

To my Little Sister, Ashley Q.,
whose own special magic brings me joy.

CHAPTER 1

The cracked sidewalks shimmered with the heat of the June sun as Sam dashed down the street, swinging a bag from the Full Belly Deli. She'd spent two nights of Mom's dinner money on it, but this was a special occasion.

Jerry behind the counter had even given her one of his fresh-baked chocolate chip cookies for free when she'd told him that today she and Mom were celebrating twelve whole months of living in Brooklyn.

Twelve months was the longest time they'd ever lived anywhere. Musicians like Mom traveled *a lot*. San Francisco. Dallas. Philadelphia. Boston.

Judy the florist smiled and plucked a daisy from her outdoor stand as Sam headed her way. She handed it to Sam and said, "You look cheery. Daisies are for cheer. Pass it on, Sam."

"Thanks!" Sam tucked it into

the grocery bag and ran into her apartment building, taking the stairs two at a time. With arms and legs burning, she passed their neighbor Mrs. Shaw with a quick "Hi!" and burst into the teeny apartment she shared with Mom.

"Ow!" She stumbled over two suitcases by the door and barely made it to the kitchen table without spilling the groceries.

Mom wasn't supposed to be home from her orchestra rehearsal for another two hours, but Sam heard her talking quietly on the phone in the bedroom they shared.

"I'll get dinner ready," Sam yelled, unpacking the bag. She boiled water and emptied a box of spaghetti into the pot, warmed up marinara sauce, steamed some broccoli, and put the garlic bread in the oven.

Please don't let me burn anything this time, she thought. She twirled around when Mom appeared, grabbing her hands and twirling her, too, her straight, blonde hair flying in one direction as Sam's black curls flew the other way.

"What's this, Samantha Sea Wells?" When Mom was surprised, she always called Sam by her full name. She often said that she loved the ocean so much that she named her daughter after it.

"We're celebrating!" Sam said, growing dizzy and stumbling. Mom laughed and pulled her down to the couch.

"It's our one-year anniversary here." Sam waited to see her mother's reaction, but she only nodded. "And now that we're staying here with your job, I can go to public school—no more homeschooling—and we can get real Christmas decorations. You know—the kind that go in a box and you pull out every December. And we can have our neighbors over for a party every year from now on. We'll call it The Get Wells Party. Get it?"

Mom sighed and let go of Sam's hand. A trickle of sweat ran down Sam's neck. The air conditioner rattled in the window, barely blowing out cold air. Christmas seemed far away.

Good, Sam thought. She wanted to be here a long time.

"I love seeing you so happy, but actually, I have something else to celebrate," Mom said. "I just got a new job."

Sam twisted her feet together. "Here?"

Mom shook her head. "I'm replacing a flutist who got sick. It's a two-month tour in Europe."

Sam jumped off the couch and stumbled into the suitcases. All of the good dinner smells suddenly didn't smell so good. "But you said New York City is the musician's capital of the world. Why would you want to tour Europe?"

"It's the opportunity of a lifetime, Sam, and it would mean a lot of money." She looked around. "I could get better jobs in New York with this on my resume."

"Can I go with you?"

Mom shook her head. "They don't have accommodations for children, and I'll be working all the time, rehearsing and playing."

Sam's nose burned as tears filled her eyes. "Where would I go for the whole summer?"

Mom stood and took Sam's hands. "With your Uncle Mitch."

Sam pulled her hands away. "I don't even know him!"

The spaghetti pot boiled over with a loud bubbling rush. Sam ran into the kitchen and turned it down, crying hard. A bitter smell filled the air. She'd forgotten to stir the marinara and had put the flame on too high.

She pulled off the lid and stirred it, but the spoon stuck to the mess on the bottom. She checked the broccoli, only to discover it had turned into a big pile of mush. She opened the oven door, and smoke poured out. The garlic bread was nothing more than a burnt brick. Dinner was ruined again.

She couldn't do anything right. Not make dinner. Not keep her new friend, Felicity. Not finally get the chance to go to public school. Not convince Mom to stay. She plopped down in a chair at the table, wiping her face.

"You spent time with Uncle Mitch and my sister, Sylvie, until you were two years old." Mom sat down across from her. "And he knows you, Sam. I send him photos and tell him about you all the time. He sends us money to help us out. He may only be your uncle by marriage, but he's still family, and he cares for you."

"But he lives so far away, in

South Carolina." Sam picked at the ripped plastic tablecloth.

"Uncle Mitch loves it there. He's got so much space in a real house. Much more than this. And the beach is right there."

"How come we've never seen him since I was two, then?"

Mom picked at the tablecloth now, not meeting her gaze. "We travel a lot, and he never leaves Foggy Harbor. He works there all the time…on special projects."

"But he's the only family we've got."

"Yes, and now it's time you got to know him." Mom smiled. "It'll be fun! You'll learn about all the famous shipwrecks and pirates off the Carolina coast from him." Her smile faltered. "Plus, there's no one else, Sam."

Certainly not Sam's dad, since he'd abandoned them when she was born. But Mom hardly ever talked about Uncle Mitch.

The daisy poked out of the grocery bag on the table. Sam pulled it out. It hung limp in her hand. "Judy says daisies are for cheer and to pass it on."

No more Judy's flower of the day. No more picking monster pickles from the barrel at the Full Belly Deli. No more making funny videos or friendship bracelets with Felicity.

"You keep it, sweetheart." Mom stood and kissed the top of her head, pulling out plates to eat their burned dinner on. "We'll be cheery again soon, Sam. I promise. We'll both go off and have our own adventures, and then we'll come back to celebrate them together."

Sam tucked the wilted daisy behind her ear and set the table. "How am I getting to Foggy Harbor?"

"I've spoken with Mrs. Shaw. She and her granddaughter Delia are heading back to their family in Myrtle Beach. You can ride the bus with them, and then you'll only have an hour by yourself between there and Foggy Harbor."

Sam stared at the suitcases sitting side by side and blew out a big sigh. "When do I leave?"

Mom strained the soggy pasta. "Tomorrow."

CHAPTER 2

Foggy Harbor, coming up," the bus driver called.

Sam clutched her backpack and stared out the dirty bus window. Dark woods had raced by for hours with only a house or farm here and there as she dozed. No one else remained on the bus but her. They'd all gotten off in big towns like Wilmington and Myrtle Beach, along with Mrs. Shaw and her granddaughter.

Delia had tried to make friends, but Sam wasn't in the mood. She'd finally given up and left Sam alone for the long bus ride.

The bus followed a curve and rolled along Main Street. All of the shops were dark, and it was only 8 p.m. A full moon cast the town in gray shadows that crept down the uneven sidewalks. On the left, the Atlantic Ocean spread like a black carpet, a wall of mist sitting heavily on the water.

In New York City, lights twinkled across Sam's ceiling all night long. She had never felt lonely there, knowing the city was awake with her. She could already tell Foggy Harbor was different. It looked like the loneliest place ever. *Why would anyone live here on purpose?* she wondered.

The driver pulled into the bus station. A neon sign that should have flashed *Foggy Harbor Parking* was missing most of its letters. BOR...ING. *Some sign,* she thought. *I'm already bored here.*

"You got someone picking you up, Miss?" the driver asked as he pulled her suitcase from the luggage

compartment. Her T-shirt clung to her in the heavy, muggy air.

Sam checked her phone for the address Mom had given her: 1 Foggy Way. "My uncle lives a block from here," she said, pointing at the street sign.

The driver nodded and pulled out of the station, leaving her under the broken sign. Sam texted Mom one word out of duty: ARRIVED.

With no choice but to find her new home, she adjusted her backpack and popped up her suitcase handle, dragging it along. It clickety-clacked all the way down the quiet street.

Uncle Mitch's stone house sat at the end, alone and secluded, hugging the ocean. Its sloped roof pierced the murky sky. One light glowed in a back window. Crickets trilled around the house, creating an eerie buzz as waves lapped the shore.

Sam crunched over the walking path made of shells, then thumped up the front porch steps and rang

the doorbell, eager to escape the empty night.

After a few minutes, the door was yanked open. A tall man with curly black hair and a bushy mustache loomed over Sam, the porch light deepening his frown. "Yes?"

Sam swallowed hard. "Uncle Mitch?"

His eyes grew wide and he pulled her inside, slamming the door. "Samantha? What are you doing here?"

Cool air washed over her from a ceiling fan that whirred above, and she shivered, shrinking under his glare. Then she remembered what Mom had said: *He's the only family we've got.* She straightened up.

"Didn't my mom tell you I was coming for the summer? She's on a music tour."

He let go of her, shaking his head, and pulled out his phone. "No, she didn't." He pointed at the couch. "Sit."

Sam sank into the couch as Uncle Mitch pressed the phone to his ear, pacing back and forth with long strides. She took the opportunity to look around.

Stacks of books littered a coffee table made from a lobster cage. There was a sagging dining room table with mismatched chairs. Oars, nets, and spears hung on the

walls like in a maritime museum she'd visited once. Shelves made of driftwood held rusty tins and antique bottles alongside watercolor paintings of islands and sailboats. The scent of saltwater and musty old things filled her nose as a breeze drifted in from the bay window that looked out over the water.

Uncle Mitch blew out a long, exasperated sigh and tossed the phone aside, placing his hands on his hips. "I can't get through to your mom." He narrowed his eyes as if that were Sam's fault. "Reception here is bad, and I misunderstood her garbled messages."

"Mom said you left a message

saying it was okay for me to come."
Sam glared right back at him.

He shook his head. "I *said*, 'I'm glad you're okay.'"

They continued to stare at each other until he dropped his arms, shoulders sagging. "Come on. I'll show you where you can sleep."

Sam grabbed her suitcase and backpack and followed him upstairs to one landing, then climbed further up a winding metal staircase. They entered a wide room with a pitched ceiling.

Uncle Mitch clicked on a ceiling fan and threw open the windows. Sea air blew away the stuffy warmth. "It's the attic, but it has its own bathroom and you can do your own thing up here."

Meaning not be with you, Sam thought. *Good. I'll find my own friends here. I'm used to starting over by myself.*

A single bed pressed up against the low eaves. A rocking chair with a quilt draped over one arm sat across from it, next to a small dresser with a lamp that let out a soft, dim glow.

An artist's easel stood in one corner, paintbrushes and bottles lining its shelf. Moonlight streamed in, casting beams across the dusty plank floors.

Uncle Mitch pulled a set of sheets from the closet and dropped them on the bed. "Tomorrow I'll contact your mom about getting you home," he said, his head nearly grazing the low ceiling.

"She's already in Europe." Panic started to set in. If Uncle Mitch sent her away, where would she go?

They stood facing each other, his gray eyes piercing hers. "You look just like your mom."

No one had ever said that to her. Uncle Mitch rubbed his chin, looking tired and not so mean for a moment, and then left.

Sam checked her phone. No cell phone bars meant no message back from Mom. She washed up in the tiny bathroom, changed into pajamas, made the bed, and slid between the cool sheets. She was exhausted from traveling all day.

She tossed in the creaky bed for what seemed like hours. As tired as she was, sleep wouldn't come. Finally, she gave up and went to the window to peer out.

The sea spread everywhere, moonlight glittering like diamonds upon it. In the distance, a wall of fog hung thick. Waves rolled to shore, lapping gently on the beach.

Movement caught her eye. Farther down the beach, a shadowy figure walked along a dock that jutted out from the shore. A small boat rocked in the water. The figure

climbed in, untied the boat, and rowed away, disappearing into the fog.

Sam crawled back into bed and dreamed of being in that rowboat, caught in a storm at sea. Her uncle yelled at her to row faster to get back home, but she had no idea where home was.

CHAPTER

3

The next morning, Sam wandered downstairs in shorts and a T-shirt to find some breakfast. She followed the smell of burnt batter to discover Uncle Mitch in the kitchen, flipping a blackened pancake. It plopped on the floor. He tugged on his hair, snatched up the pancake, and threw it in the garbage under the sink as Sam pulled out a chair at the table.

He glanced at her, bags under his eyes as if he'd been up all night, his curls as wild as hers were this morning. He pulled a plate stacked high with charred pancakes out of the oven, then placed it in front of her. "I'm not much of a cook."

That's one thing we've got in common, Sam thought as she picked up a pancake and nibbled it. "Crispy. Not bad."

"Milk?" he offered.

"I can get it." She found two glasses and filled them up. He opened the freezer and they both grabbed for ice cubes.

"Ice cold milk is the best," he said. She nodded and he sat down with her, slathering butter on his pancakes before piling blueberries on top and then drizzling maple syrup over the whole thing. They ate quietly, the tinkle of ice cubes breaking the silence as they drank.

"I still couldn't reach your mom," Uncle Mitch finally said. He looked different in the daylight and not so grumpy. His house looked different, too. The dark shadows from last night had melted away as the sun shone through clouds of mist floating outside. It made

everything look cozy and soft.

"She's in Germany," Sam said, hoping it was true. She hadn't gotten a message from Mom since she'd arrived.

Uncle Mitch nodded and stood abruptly, placing his dishes in the sink. "I'll be out back in my boatyard all day, working on a job."

Are those the "special projects" Mom mentioned? Sam wondered. Working on boats didn't seem so important. Not important enough to keep him away from his family for all these years, anyway.

Uncle Mitch wiped his hands and turned to her. "You may go to the beach or into town, but stay out of the water." He handed her a key on a ring. "Lock up when you go out. And don't get into trouble."

Nope. She'd been wrong. He was still Mr. Grumps. Sam shoved a pancake into her mouth. "I'm twelve years old and used to being alone. I've walked around big cities by myself. This is no city," she said.

Uncle Mitch fixed his gray eyes on her until she finally swallowed and looked down at her plate. "You're right, Samantha Sea Wells. This is no city, but there are darker dangers here than you can ever imagine."

With those words, he turned abruptly and left. She jumped as the screen door slammed.

Yup. Grumps, all right.

Uncle Mitch's words had sent a chill through her, but he'd remembered her full name. Perhaps Mom had been telling the truth. Maybe he had asked about her all the time. He knew about her, but she knew nothing about him.

She washed the dishes and put them in the dish rack. "Be a good guest wherever you go," Mom often said. Maybe by being neat, she'd get on Uncle Mitch's good side. If he had one.

She pulled out her phone, desperately wanting to talk to Mom. Sam's phone had one bar, and a text had come through.

Glad you made it safely, sweetheart. Miss you and love you. Uncle Mitch loves you, too. Give him a chance.

Sam typed her reply: I will, Mom. But she didn't promise, and her text failed anyway. She tried Felicity's number, but it rang once and then cut out. Frustrated, Sam turned off the phone.

A brown bird fluttered by and perched on a branch outside the kitchen window.

"Time to see what this town is all about," she said out loud. The bird chirped back at her, and Sam tucked the house key in her pocket. She checked her wallet to make sure she had the spending money Mom had given her, then trudged toward the center of town.

The humidity tightened up her curls and sat thick on her arms and neck as she passed tiny houses nestled beneath gnarled trees. Wispy moss hung down from the branches like beards. An earthy, salty smell infused the air.

She saw no one except the mail woman, who waved to her as she delivered letters. A rusty truck drove slowly through the intersection at the one stoplight in town. A dog barked in someone's backyard, and a single crow cawed overhead.

Sam felt like she was the only person awake in this sleepy town. She turned down Main Street, the ocean to her right. Fishing boats popped in and out of the blowing mist that glowed gold from the sun.

Within a few minutes, she'd taken in all the excitement Foggy Harbor had to offer: a barber shop, deli, pizza place, grocery store, post office, and bank.

She'd nearly reached the end of the block when an orange-and-white cat gave her a scratchy *meow* as it limped across her path and toward the street.

"No, kitty, don't go that way," she called. The cat stopped and looked at her. A car rumbled by as Sam took a step forward. "Here, kitty kitty."

The cat inched away, its stiff tail standing straight up. There was a spot of blood on one of its paws. It meowed louder. A door slammed nearby. The cat hunched over at the sound, and Sam took the chance to move closer. It hissed.

"Kitty, you're hurt. Let me help you."

The cat ran down the crooked sidewalk, stumbling and limping. Sam ran after it.

"Stop!" a voice called.

Sam froze. A boy about her age ran up from behind, his dark brown eyes full of concern. He wore thick gloves and held a blue blanket. The cat huddled before them, then tucked itself up against a tree on the sidewalk.

"I'm trying to help it," Sam said.

The boy shot her a serious look. "You're just scaring her," he said as he knelt, facing the cat, and pulled a small bag from his pocket.

Sam crossed her arms. "How do you know?"

"My mom's a vet and I know a lot about animals, that's how." He ripped open the bag, shook it, and said softly, "They need to come to you."

Then Sam saw the sign next to her: Foggy Harbor Veterinary Clinic, Dr. Melanie Thompson, D.V.M.

"I would have caught it and brought it to you," she said.

"It's a *she,* not an *it.*" He glanced up as she frowned at him.

"I didn't mean anything—"

"And you'd have gotten yourself all scratched up and could have hurt BooBoo even worse," he continued.

Sam uncrossed her arms and stifled a giggle. "BooBoo?"

"They call her that because she's always getting hurt. And hey, we don't name them, we just help them."

BooBoo meowed pitifully but stood up. The boy took some treats from the bag and held them out, and the cat stepped toward him.

"She's very old. We've taken care of her for years, and she's sneaky about getting out."

Her anger fading, Sam knelt beside the kid. He placed a few treats in her hand. "I'm Tuck," he said.

"Sam."

BooBoo inched forward and nibbled from Sam's hand. Sam smiled at Tuck, and he smiled back. He dropped the bag of treats into her hand and then slowly lowered the blanket over BooBoo, who was too busy munching on goodies to notice.

Tuck picked up the cat and wrapped her snugly. He held her against his chest as Sam stood with him, holding out her hand so BooBoo could finish eating.

"I've always wanted a pet, but we could never have one because we move around a lot." Sam stroked the cat, who closed her eyes sleepily and purred under Sam's touch.

"Well, you've come to the right place—my mom's office has tons."

Tuck looked down at BooBoo and frowned. "She's got a splinter in her paw. I need to get her to my mom, or it'll get infected." He glanced at Sam. "You can come too, if you want."

Sam followed Tuck around to the back of the vet office. Inside, cool air conditioning wrapped around her, and she smelled the musky scent of animals. Dogs yipped and cats cried.

A slender woman in a white coat bent over a chocolate lab on a stainless steel table. His long tail thumped sadly as she rubbed his ears. "Good boy, Chester. You'll be home in no time."

"Mom, I caught BooBoo," Tuck said. "She has a splinter in her foot."

"Thank goodness you got her!" The woman motioned toward a wooden door. "Place her in a kennel in the next room, and I'll be right in."

Tuck nodded and headed through the door.

Sam waited awkwardly, hands behind her back, but relaxed when the woman smiled down at her.

"I'm Dr. Melanie Thompson, Tuck's mom, but you can call me Mel."

"I'm Sam Wells, and I'm visiting my Uncle Mitch."

Mel nodded. "He's a wonderful boat-builder. Built most of the ones in Foggy Harbor."

Tuck returned empty-handed. "All set, Mom. Oh, this is Sam. She helped me catch BooBoo."

"We've met, and thank you for that, Sam," Mel said. "Why don't you two go have fun? I'm covered for the day, Tuck, and it's summer, after all."

On a whim, Sam said, "We could hang out at my uncle's house, if you want. It's by the beach."

"I know right where it is," Mel said, nodding.

Tuck shrugged. "Sure." He reached over to pet Chester. "No more grapes for you, gilly soose." The dog licked his hand. Tuck grinned at Sam's puzzled expression as they walked out the back door. "I like to switch up those words," he explained.

"Silly goose. Got it," she said, grinning back. "What happened to Chester?"

"He ate grapes. They can cause kidney failure and kill a dog."

"I never liked grapes, anyways."

Tuck laughed. "Me neither. I'm more of a cherries man."

"They definitely go better with ice cream."

"And hot fudge."

They laughed together.

Sam felt a rush of happiness. Suddenly, Foggy Harbor didn't seem so boring.

CHAPTER

4

After getting lunch at the deli and then sharing a hot fudge sundae with cherries on top, Sam and Tuck took the long way back to Uncle Mitch's house, down the beach walk.

No longer the ghost town it had seemed like the night before,

Foggy Harbor was now full of people who popped out of their houses to garden or walk their dogs. It took Sam and Tuck forever to get back because everyone knew Tuck and wanted to chat about their dog or cat, or to congratulate him on winning the sixth-grade science fair.

The fog finally disappeared from the town, but it still hung strangely in a heavy cloud out to sea. It sat directly across from the harbor, hunkered down like an enormous cloak.

"Why isn't that disappearing?" Sam asked, pointing at the fog.

"They call it Lost Luck," Tuck said.

"How come?"

"Because there are tales of unlucky people heading into it and never coming back."

A shiver ran through Sam, even as the warm afternoon sun shone down.

"Every fishing boat knows to go around it."

"That's so weird." Sam kicked shells along the edge of the path as they walked, the hulking fog bank unmoving.

Tuck shrugged. "It's been here forever." He glanced sideways at her. "Legend has it, creatures rule whatever's hidden in that fog."

Sam stopped kicking shells and

stared at him. "Like mermaids, or something?"

"Nope." He lowered his voice. "Sea monsters."

Finally, they reached the edge of town and Uncle Mitch's house. The whirr of a buzz saw greeted them from his boatyard in the back. In daylight, Sam could see the sign hanging off the tree in front: Mitch Mardock, Boat Builder.

"Cool," Tuck said as they stepped inside the house. He studied the mix of nautical stuff on the walls. "Wow! These nets are handmade. Their knots are all uneven, and they're made from silk, not nylon." He shook his head in amazement.

"They stopped making nets like these at least a hundred years ago."

Sam looked at the nets with new respect and pulled Tuck along, getting a whiff of sawdust blowing in from the boatyard. "Let's see what else we can find."

In a walk-in pantry off the kitchen they discovered a tackle box with homemade fishing hooks and an old metal Muller's Dairy milk jug full of seashells. Tuck explained the differences between clam, mussel, scallop, and oyster shells. "Your uncle probably collects them to grind up for his walkway."

"How do you know so much stuff?" Sam asked.

"I like to read about the history and science of where I live. Don't you?" He turned a shell over in his hand.

Sam had never thought about it. "Mom and I move every six months or so to a new city where she plays in the orchestra, so I don't get to know a place for that long."

Tuck's eyes widened. "That's so exciting. I've lived here all my life. Nothing changes."

As they walked back into the living room, the whirring out back got louder. They peered through the window to a fenced-in backyard. Uncle Mitch wore safety goggles as he bent over wooden boards on a workbench, sawing them into pieces.

Sawdust collected at his feet.

"Your uncle's family has been around here the longest," Tuck said. "They've lived in this house since the Revolutionary War."

Sam knitted her brow. "You mean *my* family."

Tuck pulled back from the window. "Sorry. That's what I meant. It's just that your uncle never mentioned having a family since his wife died."

Sam's mouth fell open. "He never mentioned us *at all*?"

Tuck shook his head. "Mom said his wife died when I was two."

That was probably the reason they hadn't visited Uncle Mitch since she was two, either. "Maybe Uncle Mitch seems mean, when he's really just sad," she said.

"For sure," said Tuck.

As they turned to go, Sam tripped on a faded blue area rug. When she bent to flatten it back down, she saw the gleam of a black metal hinge poking out. She pulled back the rug.

"Look, a hidden trap door!" Sam yanked up on the handle to open the door, revealing steps spiraling down into a dark space. Glancing around, she spied a flashlight on a shelf. She grabbed it and headed down into the darkness.

"Wait," Tuck said. "Shouldn't we ask your uncle if it's okay?"

"This is my family's house, so isn't it mine, too?" Sam asked. Her heart was racing—she wanted to explore.

Tuck scrunched up his face, thinking, then reluctantly nodded.

As Sam climbed down, a rich wooden scent filled the air, and she heard a faint ticking sound. She stepped onto a smooth stone floor and flashed the light around. The room was cool and dry and paneled with wood.

"It's lined with cedar, to prevent moths," Tuck said, coming down behind her. He yanked on a chain and a lightbulb flashed on, swaying above them. "There's a thermostat down here," he said, pointing to a light blinking in one corner. "It's climate controlled."

Sam turned the flashlight on him. "What's so exciting about that?"

Tuck held a hand over his eyes, and Sam lowered the flashlight. "Maybe your uncle has a humidity and air-conditioning system down here because there's super important stuff he doesn't want ruined, like documents or antiques."

"I would rather have AC in the house than in the basement," Sam grumbled.

"Summer isn't usually this hot here. Foggy Harbor is actually the coolest place on the South Carolina coast." Tuck picked up what looked like an animal horn from a shelf.

"What's that?" Sam asked.

Tuck held it under the light. "No idea." They bumped heads leaning in to investigate. The pale gray horn gleamed. It was shaped like a soft-serve ice cream twist, thinner at the top and thicker at the base.

There were horns of different sizes on the shelf, along with several hanks of white hair tied together with ribbon, some brushes, and large metal nail files.

"Why don't you know, gilly soose?" Sam teased.

Tuck put the horn back, but he didn't laugh. "We should go. This place is private."

Sam ignored him and pulled a strange, tall metal box off one shelf. It was the source of the ticking. "Cool," she said.

Tuck leaned in, his eyes bright with curiosity. "It's a clock."

The front was made of glass. Outside the case hung a key. At the top, a round, yellowed face displayed Roman numerals one through twenty-four, with the hands pointing to the correct time of 5:30 p.m. But the clock also had square windows cut out around the face that read "Three-quarters full," "Half-full," "One-quarter full," and "Empty." The window for three-quarters full was colored red.

Below the face, a pendulum swung back and forth.

"I wonder what it measures," Tuck said.

A flash of metal caught Sam's eye. Etched onto a delicate brass plate at the bottom of the clock were the words *Fog clock.*

"Why would you need a clock to tell fog time?" Sam asked. "For that matter, what *is* fog time?"

Tuck grabbed the flashlight from her, squinting hard. "There's tiny script below the title." He read it to Sam: "Whosoever is named fog keeper must endeavor to keep this clock in good working order and wound for all days and nights, passing it on to the next fog keeper when their time is done. Whosoever breaks this trust breaks the honor of the role of fog keeper and therefore breaks the magic."

Sam inhaled sharply, gripping Tuck's sleeve. They looked at each other with wonder.

"What does it mean?" she whispered, the clock's ticking vibrating through her.

"It means that your uncle is a fog keeper," he said.

CHAPTER

5

Tuck and Sam stared at the clock.

"So, he keeps Foggy Harbor foggy with this? But how, and why?" Sam asked.

Tuck shook his head, and together, they placed the clock back on the shelf.

Above them, the hammering had quit, and they heard Uncle Mitch's buzz saw start up again.

"Let's get out of here before your uncle finds us," Tuck said, heading for the stairs. But Sam was already exploring other corners of the hidden room.

One shelf held dusty bottles of murky liquid with peeling labels on them, their names too faded to read.

Another shelf held a long, wooden spear with a sharp metal arrow tip lashed on with rope. This one didn't look old, like the whale harpoon upstairs. It looked new and polished, like it had been recently handmade.

"Come on, Sam," Tuck said.

But she shook her head. Moving around with Mom, who didn't talk about the past, Sam never had any mementos—no family photos, nothing to prove that she'd come from somewhere.

Now, here was a room full of secret treasures carrying loads of clues to her past, and Uncle Mitch could answer them all. She flipped open a trunk, pulling out a handful of white lace. A wedding dress. "I bet this was his wife's dress," she said.

Sam dug further into the trunk as Tuck walked over to the staircase, ready to head up. At the bottom of the chest sat a small box. Sam opened it. A bunch of letters tied with a red ribbon filled the box.

Tucked sighed and came over as Sam undid the ribbon. They unfolded the top letter together, and Sam read it aloud.

My Darling Sylvie,

Each day our special place beckons. I never knew such love could carry such hope. When we roam our wild, magical island together, I want to stay forever. Now that you know the truth, we must protect this wondrous and terrible secret. I no longer suffer alone. It is now our burden, but it's made lighter through you.

Always, with love,

Mitchell

Sam ran a finger over the crinkled paper, her chest bursting with emotion over all that Uncle Mitch had lost. "What island is he writing about, Tuck?"

"There aren't any islands here," he said. "The nearest one is miles away."

Sam fished around the bottom of the box for more clues and pulled out a creased photo of a woman wearing a wedding dress on a beach. Tall, green trees and giant ferns swayed in the background. She clasped a bunch of sunflowers, tilting her head with a soft smile.

"Sam, you two have the same face!" Tuck said.

It was like looking at an older version of herself. The woman had the same upturned nose and large brown eyes. Apart from her long, blonde hair, she looked just like Sam.

Sam flipped the photo over. Across the back, someone had scrawled *Sylvie Mardock*.

Silence filled the hidden room. The buzz saw and hammering had stopped. Sam froze. A screen door

slammed. She gripped the photo, then quickly slid it into her shorts pocket.

Feet stomped down the stairs.

Uncle Mitch loomed over her, blocking the light. "What are you doing?" he yelled, grabbing the letters from her hands.

"We were…just exploring," Sam said.

Tuck hung his head. Uncle Mitch pointed at him. "You, Tucker Thompson, are a snoop. You instigated this, didn't you?"

Tuck's head shot up. "No! I… I didn't, Mr. Mardock."

"Get out." Uncle Mitch rose taller, his head nearly bumping the ceiling.

"He didn't do anything!" Sam shouted. "He didn't want to come down here. I made him do it."

Uncle Mitch pointed to the stairs. "Now!" His voice boomed in the small room.

Tuck darted his eyes at Sam. "Sorry," he mumbled and ran up the stairs.

Her one new friend, gone. Before she could say anything, Uncle Mitch turned to her, clutching the letters. "That boy is never to come into my house again."

"He's my friend," Sam said, feeling lost and wishing with every part of her that she could be back with Mom in Brooklyn. They could be eating ice cream cones in the park right now.

Uncle Mitch turned away from her, set the letters on a shelf, and carefully tied the ribbon back around them. He put the bundle of letters into the box and placed it in the trunk. Then he knelt and gently folded the wedding dress, placing it on top of the box of letters. He quietly closed the trunk, resting his hands on it.

"What is this room?" Sam asked. "Why are all of these things down here, and why do you have a—"

"Tomorrow we will find somewhere else for you to go." Uncle Mitch's shoulders slumped.

Sam tried another way. "I promise we won't come down here anymore. Can't I please have Tuck over and—"

"No!" He banged a hand on the top of the trunk, his shoulders shaking. "And you can't stay. It's not safe."

"Afraid I'll discover your secrets?" she asked. Ditched again. "You're the worst uncle ever!" She bolted for the stairs, then looked back. "Mom was wrong about you. You don't care about me at all!"

Sam reached the top of the stairs and threw the trapdoor down. She ran upstairs to the attic and slammed the door, shaking the frame, then fell on the bed.

She cried hard, rocking back and forth as she let all of her anger spill out. When her sobs finally subsided, she rolled over and stared up at the ceiling. The photo she'd snuck upstairs poked out from her pocket. She pulled it out and studied Uncle Mitch's dead wife—her aunt—who looked like her.

Mom rarely mentioned their relatives. "I've lost most of my family, but that's in the past, and now I have you," she'd often say.

I need you, Mom. Sam crossed her fingers and turned on her phone. Finally, a text!

In Frankfurt. Rehearsals went well. Love and miss you. Wish you were here.

"No, you don't, or you'd have found a way to bring me with you," Sam said to the sea air that blew in.

A salty breeze kissed her goodnight as she curled up under the covers, holding the photo of someone lost, feeling the exact same way.

She cried herself to sleep, wishing the lonely away.

Sam woke to a full moon gazing down at her through the window. Her stomach rumbled. She'd gone to bed so early that she hadn't eaten dinner.

The photo of Aunt Sylvie lay beside her pillow. She slid it back into her pocket and listened to the old house creak and groan. She didn't hear Uncle Mitch moving around downstairs. *Good,* she thought.

She checked the time on her phone. It was midnight. *I'll sneak downstairs, grab some food, and avoid him,* she thought. As she sat up, she heard the splashing of water. She tiptoed over and scanned the sea. More splashes filled the silence between lapping waves.

Just offshore, a figure rowed a boat through the ocean, bobbing in and out of the billowing mist. Sam recognized the tilt of that head and those hunched-over shoulders:

Uncle Mitch. He was headed for the fog bank, but it looked different. Part of the fog had lifted, and a dark shape rose from the water where it had cleared. A hidden island!

Sam strained her eyes to take in the magic of this mysterious form, but the fog fell over it, and the island disappeared.

She gripped the windowsill, waiting for it to show itself again. But it remained hidden as she watched Uncle Mitch row away on a sliver of moonlight, wishing he'd disappear into the fog bank and never come back.

CHAPTER

6

Sam woke just as the sun cleared the horizon and peeked into her room. She washed up and headed slowly downstairs. No sign of Uncle Mitch. No work noises coming from the boatyard.

An uneasy feeling came over her

as she remembered Uncle Mitch rowing toward the island. Maybe she had really imagined it. Sam looked around the kitchen for a note, but found none. *Why would he leave me a note?* she thought. *He plans to send me away today.*

She could at least make herself a good going-away breakfast, wherever "away" might be. She pulled out bowls, a wooden spoon, eggs, and flour, and soon she had pancakes sizzling in a buttered frying pan.

She fished around in the freezer and found some sausage. She threw that in another pan, turning up the heat all the way, since it was frozen.

Mom would say, "Got fruit?" she thought.

Sam didn't see any blueberries in the kitchen, so she headed to the pantry. The rug was smoothed down and in place over the trapdoor.

She lingered, wanting to go down there again—but not without Tuck, and not if Uncle Mitch was going to come back and find her again.

His words came back to her. *It's not safe.* What did that even mean? This was the quietest town ever. No "darker dangers" lurked here.

Or did they? Maybe there was more to this sleepy town than she thought. Or maybe being all alone had made her uncle a bit crazy. She resisted the urge to go down to the secret room and instead searched until she found a bowl of blueberries in the pantry cupboard. But back in the kitchen, bitter smoke filled the air. She dashed in, dropping blueberries on the floor, and turned off the stove top. Burned again. She sat down and gnawed on her

unsatisfying, charred breakfast while she listened for Uncle Mitch.

As the minutes ticked by, a terrifying thought struck her: What if she really *did* cause her uncle to disappear? Her wishes didn't always come true, but what if they did in Foggy Harbor?

Sam shook her head, trying to clear the thought from her mind. She needed to see a friendly face, so she quickly cleaned up and headed to the vet's office.

Tuck nodded to her from behind a desk as she entered. The waiting room was empty, but yips and meows filled the back rooms where patients recovered.

"Can you take a break?" Sam asked, stuffing her hands in her pockets, desperately hoping he still wanted to be friends.

He grinned, and she knew everything was okay. He slid some folders into a filing cabinet. "Sure, we're not busy today."

He turned to a woman who was tallying receipts behind the counter. "Nancy, is it all right if I hang out with Sam?"

Nancy waved them out. "Go have fun, kiddos. I'll watch the front and let your mom know."

They walked down Main Street under a gray sky. Sam took a deep breath. "I'm sorry about the way that

Uncle Mitch treated you. I bet he didn't mean it."

Tuck laughed. "It's okay. We shouldn't have been down there and, according to Mom, he's always been crabby. She said it's because he lives alone, like a hermit." He slowed. "Well, that and because his wife disappeared."

"What happened?" Sam asked as they turned a corner next to the harbor. A gust of wind blew across the water, rocking the boats as mist drifted between them.

Tuck stopped, thinking about that. "No one knows. She left one day and didn't return. There was an investigation, but they didn't find anything. My mom said your uncle never got over her and locked himself away from the world."

"That's crazy," Sam said as they walked on.

"Yeah. Maybe you should ask him what happened."

"I can't." She pulled him to a stop. "Uncle Mitch disappeared, too."

Tuck cocked his head, looking doubtful. "How?"

Sam hadn't realized how worried she was until the words came rushing out of her. "I saw him row off in a boat last night, and he never came back."

Tuck's eyes grew wide. "Are you sure?"

She nodded, then leaned in. "He was headed for Lost Luck."

Sailboats in the harbor clapped their sails in the wind, and Tuck jumped with the sound. "He wouldn't go into the fog."

"It's not just fog, Tuck," Sam said, the words coming so fast they ran together. "There's an island behind it. I saw it!"

Tuck shook his head, opened and closed his mouth, and then finally said, "There's no island, Sam. It's not on any map. Believe me, I've looked."

"But what about the letter we found? It mentions a magical island."

Tuck shrugged. "That doesn't mean the island is here. It could be halfway across the world, for all we know."

An elderly man walked past with his dog and gave them a wave. Tuck smiled at him and then frowned at Sam. "Look, I know you aren't getting along with your uncle, but—"

Sam threw her arms high into the air. "I wished him away, Tuck. I did. I wished he'd vanish into the fog bank and never come back. And now he's gone!"

Tuck shook his head. "You can't wish someone away."

She lowered her hands. It did sound ridiculous. "Okay, maybe not.

But there *is* an island there. Trust me. I'll show you."

Tuck looked at the harbor. "My house has a good view of the fog bank, and I have a boat. *If* we see it, I'll take you there."

Sam sprinted ahead. "Turn left at the corner," Tuck called after her. He soon caught up and they ran together.

Sam's heart was pounding and full of hope. Tuck would see the island and believe her, they'd bring Uncle Mitch back, and she'd never wish anyone away ever again.

Tuck's house sat on a corner at the end of a long street. It was right near the edge of the harbor.

"That's my room, right up there." He pointed at a window with blue curtains peeking out against the sunny yellow house.

It was cozy inside the bungalow, with plump couches and chairs, lace curtains, and bright oil paintings of flowers. Sam loved it right away.

Tuck led her through to the back of the house, where a porch wrapped around. Stepping out of the sliding doors, they had a clear view of the harbor. Fog blew across it, but the sun broke through in patches.

A motorboat, kayak, and rowboat

were tied to a dock that jutted out just beyond Tuck's tiny back lawn. On the right, the ocean spread far and wide. Lost Luck rose tall across from them, its round, gray dome squatting on the ocean.

"Sam, there's nothing—"

She clutched the porch post. "Just wait and see."

For a long while, they gazed at the fog bank. It seemed as solid and immovable as a house as it sat there, hiding the island Sam knew was behind it.

Tuck flopped down in a chair. "Sorry, Sam, but I don't see it."

Neither did she. Tears pricked her eyes.

"It was night when you thought you saw an island, right?"

She nodded, biting her lip to keep from crying. "I did *not* make it up." Her eyes burned as she stared at Lost Luck without blinking, willing it to show them the island she'd seen.

"I don't think you made it up, but it was dark and there were shadows. Maybe you just wanted to see something there," he said quietly.

"But if there's no island, where did Uncle Mitch go? And why hasn't he come back?"

Tuck didn't answer.

Sam jerked around to look at him. "Maybe the fog clock has something to do with it. If he's whatever a fog keeper is…?" She trailed off, not sure what being a fog keeper even meant.

"I looked it up," Tuck said. "A fog keeper used to keep the foghorn going when it was too foggy to see the lighthouse light. But no one's had that job in a hundred years."

Sam tapped a foot. "I know there's an island out there, and I'm pretty sure my uncle's stuck on it."

Tuck just frowned and shook his head.

"You don't believe me, but I know it's there. I'll prove it to you!" Sam yanked open the sliding doors and ran through the house, ignoring Tuck's calls to come back.

CHAPTER

7

Sam stayed holed up in her room all afternoon and evening, watching the sea from her window. She ate a sandwich and some grapes for dinner, which made her think of poor sick Chester the lab, which made her think of her argument with Tuck.

The fog bank never moved. If Uncle Mitch didn't come back tonight, she'd have to persuade Tuck to take her in his boat to look for him.

Over and over, she dialed Mom's number, but each of her calls got disconnected. She was almost ready to give up when she heard Mom's voice saying hello. Her call had gotten through!

"Mom! I'm so glad you picked up. Uncle Mitch is gone!"

"That's great that Mitch is fun."

"That's not what I said!"

Mom's words weaved in and out, garbled, and then she was gone. Sam tried calling again, but her cell reception was back to zero.

The sun sank lower, then slipped below the horizon. She shivered as the temperature sank, fog moving heavily across the distant harbor and enclosing it.

She wrapped the quilt around herself and rocked by the window, watching the moon rise. Stars winked above as the sky grew dark.

Eventually, Sam dozed, but she jerked awake every time the wind whipped off the water with a great howl. The old house groaned as branches from the oak trees lashed at it. The walls creaked and sighed. Sam stood to stretch her aching back and looked out the window into the darkness.

The fog bank had lifted! The island stabbed toward the sky, dark and eerie, floating on the ocean. A mountain rose from the center, its ridges sloping downward toward the sea.

Why would the island be visible now? Sam wondered. When she had

wanted Tuck to see it, the island had not appeared. And up until now, no one in Foggy Harbor had ever seen it.

Two words floated into her head: *fog clock*. She ran down the stairs, opened the trapdoor, and grabbed the clock from its shelf in the hidden room. The hands on the face showed the time at the final number, twenty-four, and the window below it was colored red. Empty. What could that mean?

Empty things could be trouble. A car with no gas. A water bottle. A stomach. She didn't know what empty meant here, but she knew it could be something bad, and that could be what was preventing Uncle Mitch from getting home.

She placed the clock back on the shelf, scrambled up the winding stairs, and ran all the way to Tuck's house. The wind had stilled, and the air was heavy and hushed. The only sounds on the darkened streets were singing crickets and the slap of her feet on the pavement.

Tuck's house shone sunny yellow in the bright moonlight. Searching their driveway, Sam found a small piece of oyster shell and tossed it at his bedroom window. It hit with a clatter. Nothing. She found another and tossed it, too.

Tuck appeared and pushed up

his window. "What are you doing?" he whispered.

"The island appeared, Tuck!" She jumped up and down. "Come see."

Tuck rubbed his eyes, then nodded. "Meet me out back."

She snuck through the gate, fidgeting until he quietly slid out onto the porch wearing jeans and a T-shirt. He froze when he saw the island, then stumbled toward the porch post, gripping it. "Wow, you were right, Sam."

They gazed at it together. "It's huge," he said. "And it's been there this whole time."

"I checked the fog clock," Sam said. "It's on empty."

Tuck nodded slowly as Sam went on. "If my uncle's the fog keeper, then maybe without him here, the fog will disappear and the island won't stay hidden."

Tuck tore his gaze from the island and looked toward her, his face lit with the moonlight. "But why does it need to be hidden?"

"Because of whatever they were talking about in the letter. It said that Uncle Mitch and Sylvie must protect this wondrous and terrible secret."

Tuck nodded furiously, tapping his fingers on the post. "The island is a secret and there's something on it that needs to stay hidden."

"Only he's stuck on it," Sam said. "We've got to help him."

"Come on." He grabbed her hand and they ran down toward the dock.

Tuck got in the front of the rowboat, grabbing two life jackets from a box in the middle. They both put them on. He showed Sam how to slide the oars into the oarlocks, and they rowed out of the harbor.

It took Sam a bit, but she finally got the hang of rowing and was soon in sync with Tuck.

With each dip and splash of the oars, they moved closer to the island. The wind picked up as they got farther from the harbor, and soon they were surrounded by the open sea.

"I wish I had an island," Sam whispered to the wind and waves as the island loomed larger before them. *If I did, Mom and I could live*

there forever and we'd never leave, she thought.

They cut through a faint mist, rowing faster toward the island's shore. Arms aching, Sam glanced up quickly to watch Foggy Harbor's streetlights softly twinkle and grow smaller.

Ahead, a sandy beach lined the island. Trees with pale green leaves rose behind it, covering the jagged mountain that watched over them.

The boat slid onto the beach, and they yanked off their life jackets. Tuck jumped out and Sam followed, pulling the boat up onto the sand near Uncle Mitch's boat, which was tied to a tree.

"I don't have any rope," said Tuck, "but it should be okay."

Wind blew through the tall green trees. Ferns with giant fronds waved, parting to reveal a path. This was the same beach where the photo of Aunt Sylvie was taken!

"That's where we go," Sam said, pointing at the path. She was already headed for the woods when Tuck pulled her back. He pointed up. From over the mountain, a dark-winged figure flew their way, its eyes fixed on them as it soared closer. With a *whoosh* it circled around, pulled in its wings, and set down on the beach.

"A flying monster!" Tuck said, yanking Sam back toward the boat, but she dragged her feet in the sand, unable to look away from the creature.

Covered in gray scales, its long snout quivered as it twitched its pointy ears and flicked its long, spine-covered, arrow-tipped tail. Around its neck hung a silver necklace with a curl of white hair. The beast stomped its clawed feet, flapped its wings, and tilted its head as if inspecting them.

"It's a dragon!" Sam said, clutching Tuck back.

The so-called dragon stomped its feet again.

"We'll be charred to bits," Tuck whispered.

The creature shook its head with

a snort and shot out a great white blast from its mouth. It froze the ferns beside it, covering them in frost.

"I guess this dragon...only *freezes* things?" Sam said, taking a step forward.

The creature puffed out its chest and glared at her, as if wanting to correct her.

"Maybe it can help us find my Uncle Mitch."

Upon hearing that, the creature stood taller and nodded.

"Can you take us to my uncle?" Sam looked at the magical creature in awe. Not only did he exist, but he also seemed to understand her!

The beast nodded again and showed its teeth, zipping a tongue in and out.

"He's smiling at us," Sam said.

"Or he's hungry and his dinner just showed up," Tuck whispered.

Sam shook her head as the creature turned and headed for the path, walking on clawed feet and the tips of his wings.

"Come on!" Sam ran after the creature, careful not to tread on its spiny tail. Tuck groaned but quickly fell in beside her as they entered the woods.

Lightning bugs unlike any they'd seen before glowed with soft blue light, darting above the ferns.

Round, red flowers bloomed low to the ground, while fragrant orange plants as tall as Sam grew along the path, glowing in shafts of moonbeams. Sam ran her fingers over their strange leaves as she trotted to keep up with the ice-breathing beast.

The creature stopped and *tap-tapped* a wing to the ground with urgency, as if to say, "Hurry up!"

"Don't want to annoy a dragon," Tuck said to Sam. The creature actually rolled its eyes at them, and they ran faster.

Soon the forest fell away and they found themselves in a wide meadow at the foot of the mountain.

In the distance, what appeared to be white horses roamed, eating the grass.

"How did horses get on this island?" Tuck asked as they stepped into the meadow, the cool grass tickling their legs.

Sam slowed, then stopped. "I don't know, but maybe they can help us," she said, staring at the creatures.

Tuck froze beside her. "What do you mean?"

The creature motioned with its wings for them to follow him across the meadow and then took off.

Sam took Tuck's hand in hers. "We came here to find my uncle. The dragon seems to know him and is helping. They could, too."

In the distance, the white beasts saw them and reared up, pawing the air.

Tuck nodded, squeezing Sam's hand.

As they walked forward, the animals began to gallop around the meadow. They gleamed pearly white in the mist, each with a spiral horn protruding from its forehead.

"Unicorns!" Sam and Tuck yelled together, both jerking to a stop.

Samantha Sea Wells, we've been expecting you.

Sam heard the words clearly in her head. Goosebumps pricked her arms. Were they speaking to her, or had she imagined it?

As she and Tuck crept closer, the herd parted to reveal a large, three-sided stone hut on the edge of the meadow, smoke curling up from a hole in its roof.

"It looks like they're protecting something there," Sam said.

The winged creature snorted down at them as if to say, "It's about time you got something right."

CHAPTER

8

Inside the hut, a man bent over beside a fire, a bowl in his hands.

Uncle Mitch!

Sam ran as fast as she could, happier than she could have imagined to see her grumpy uncle. He looked tired, but unhurt.

The unicorns outside the hut whinnied and tore up the ground, but they let her pass. As she entered the hut, she saw that Uncle Mitch was bent over a baby unicorn lying on a bed of leaves, its tiny body struggling to breathe.

Uncle Mitch jerked his head up when he heard her come in, then rushed to set the bowl down and meet her halfway with one long stride. To her surprise, he embraced her, his hug big and comforting. He smelled like straw and earth.

"Sam, how did you find me?" He pulled away with a tense look, shadows from the fire streaking his face.

"I stayed up all night watching for you to come back across the sea, and the fog finally lifted to show us the island." Tuck came up behind her. "Tuck brought us here in his boat."

Uncle Mitch blew out a big sigh, scratching his scruffy chin. "I'm sorry if I worried you. I knew the fog clock was running low, but if I'd gone home, this little one would have died." He glanced at the baby unicorn, then peered down at the children with exhausted eyes. He put a hand on Sam's shoulder. "I'm sorry I couldn't return."

"I thought I'd wished you away and you'd be gone forever," Sam said, the words tumbling out.

Uncle Mitch smiled and looked kindly at her. "I don't blame you for wishing that. I'm sorry I yelled at you." He put his other hand on Tuck's shoulder. "Both of you. Thank you for coming."

Tuck smiled shyly.

Uncle Mitch knelt by the baby unicorn's side. "Barloc's very sick. He was born last night and hasn't even been able to stand yet."

"You name the unicorns?" Sam asked.

"Yes, a name is important." He placed a hand on the creature's neck, stroking it softly. "Barloc means 'strong warrior filled with hope.' It's what the island needs."

A grown unicorn approached the front of the hut, rushing in to rub horns with Barloc, then dashing away again.

"That's Barloc's mother's friend, Truad. She's very upset because Barloc's mother died last night while giving birth to him." Uncle Mitch bent his head to the baby unicorn. "Only one unicorn is born every century. They live a long time. Barloc's mother has gone too soon."

"Are the horns and the tails in your hidden room from all the unicorns that died?" Sam asked.

"Yes," he said, listening to Barloc's chest. "When a unicorn dies, it fades away, and all that remains is its horn and a lock of hair from its tail. I inherited the ones you saw from the fog keepers before me."

Barloc chuffed in distress.

You miss your mother, too, a voice spoke inside Sam's head. Barloc strained to lift his head and gaze into Sam's eyes.

How can you know that? Sam thought, staring into his deep violet eyes.

We sense all within and are born with the memories of our ancestors.

I'm sorry your mother won't come back, Sam thought.

Don't fear, yours will.

Sam shrugged. *I know she will. I'm not afraid of that.*

Your real mother, I mean.

Barloc dropped his head and closed his eyes, his words leaving Sam stunned. What had he meant? How could he know anything about her family? She wasn't sure what to think or believe.

While her thoughts raced, Uncle Mitch began singing softly to Barloc.

A long time ago, you beheld magic from sky and star

While embracing green and sun and all that is pure.

We wished to believe—but all could not see what you are,

A beauty and kindness that can forever endure.

Help me now, keep you safe and strong

So forever on earth we may live without fear and wrong.

Sam knelt beside him, her heart filled with wonder. Mom had been right. They both had gone off to have adventures. Sam just wished she could share this with her now.

"Barloc's heart is racing too fast," Uncle Mitch said, smoothing down the unicorn's mane. "He can't breathe deeply because of it. Song soothes him some, and I've made him a drink of sparkling stream water, starlight berries, and crushed melody plant leaves. It should make him stronger, but he's not getting any better."

Tuck knelt, too. "Are unicorns like horses?" he asked.

Uncle Mitch nodded a little.

"I know a little about horses from my mom. Grooming them lowers their heart rate and calms them down."

"You're a smart boy, Tucker," Uncle Mitch said. "Quick, grab that big brush in the corner and help us."

Sam got the brush and handed it to Tuck. He began gently grooming the baby unicorn. Its breathing calmed a bit.

Uncle Mitch retrieved his bowl and placed it by the unicorn's head. "Lift his head, Sam."

Barloc sipped the drink, his pearly horn reflecting flames from the fire, then closed his eyes. Truad returned, folded her legs, and laid beside him, their horns touching.

"Can unicorns heal with their horns?" Sam asked.

"They can only heal others, not themselves," Uncle Mitch said.

The flying creature, who had been circling like a lookout, dropped down and curled up in front of the hut like a massive, gray-scaled boulder. He wrapped his long tail around himself and stared at them with bright eyes.

Uncle Mitch placed a wool blanket over the baby unicorn. He added a log to the fire and sat against the hut's stone wall. Tuck and Sam leaned back against a pile of hay.

"You must have many questions," Uncle Mitch said, folding his hands in his lap and gazing intently at Sam and Tuck.

Tuck spoke up. "Did you name the dragon, too?"

"No," Uncle Mitch laughed, and it echoed off the stone walls. "Dragon names are secret to them." The creature popped his head up with a frown and tapped his tail on the ground, the spines standing up. "Also, he's no dragon. He's a wyvern."

The wyvern stopped tapping, and his spines relaxed. He stuck out his tongue at Sam and Tuck as if to say, *So there* before he settled his head back down.

Sam said it out loud, slowly, never having heard of such a creature. "Why-vern."

"That's right. Wyverns are

smaller and have two legs. Dragons have four," Uncle Mitch explained to Sam and Tuck's puzzled expressions. "They have sharper teeth and claws, and they breathe frost, not fire."

The wyvern's tail spines shot up again as he glared at Uncle Mitch and stabbed the ground with the point of his tail.

"Oh, sorry," Uncle Mitch said with a bow to the wyvern. "They're also much faster flyers than dragons."

The wyvern grinned and settled back down with a huff, satisfied.

"Well, this wyvern needs a name," Sam said. She went to the wyvern and rubbed under his chin. He chittered as if tickled, closing his eyes with a sigh. "I'm calling him Verny."

He popped one eye open but didn't seem to object. Then he rolled over like a dog, kicking his feet in the air. Sam laughed and scratched his scaly belly. The unicorns stopped grazing and shook their manes and whinnied as if they were laughing, too.

The night grew colder, and Sam shivered. Uncle Mitch put more wood on the fire and gave her and Tuck each a wool blanket.

"If this baby is not better before sunrise, I'll need you two to get back to the mainland and wind the fog clock," he told them. "You'll have to hide the island before Foggy Harbor wakes up and sees it. Take the key on the case and put it in the hole on the face. Wind it up until the short hand is on twenty-four again. Will you do that?"

Sam and Tuck nodded together, then both started talking at once, all of their questions tumbling out.

Uncle Mitch held up his hands to quiet them. "I will tell you all I know."

CHAPTER

9

Sam, Tuck, and Uncle Mitch settled back under their blankets, the stars shining down from a clear night sky. When Uncle Mitch began to talk, even Verny turned his head as if he were listening, and the unicorn herd trotted over and stood in front of the hut.

"Centuries ago, during medieval times, unicorns roamed the earth. However, they were hunted nearly to extinction for the healing powers of their horns.

"My ancestor, Edward Oakes, was a scientist who adored these creatures. He led the unicorns here and created the fog clock to keep the island hidden with magic, becoming the first fog keeper to guard the unicorns. The fog clock has been handed down through the generations ever since, until it reached me."

He paused as Sam and Tuck digested his story. *Unicorn protectors*, thought Sam with excitement. *What I wouldn't give to be one.*

Uncle Mitch continued. "I wind the clock each day and come here each night to check on the unicorns." He swept his hand out. "Verny, as you now call him, happened to be sleeping on the island when Oakes first shielded it. Verny liked the unicorns so much, he decided to stick around indefinitely."

They all looked at Verny, who lifted his head and eyed Uncle Mitch. "You could say he's a second protector to the unicorns, when I'm not here. He even wears an ancient lock of unicorn hair around his neck as a sign."

Verny nodded and flicked his tongue. He shook the bundle of white hairs on his necklace and then settled back down in the grass, his scales shining silver in the firelight.

"Unicorns allow us to discover more about the world than we could ever know without them," Uncle Mitch said, gazing at the herd beyond the fire.

"How?" Sam asked.

He turned to her. "They help us believe that magic is real, and in believing, we can unleash our own magical potential."

He rose then to check on Barloc, and Sam and Tuck glanced at each other. Sam understood now why her uncle had gotten so angry at them for going into the hidden room. He wanted to keep the unicorns safe. So did she.

The fire popped, sending up sparks.

"Who's going to guard the island when...when you're not fog keeper anymore?" Sam asked. Tuck nudged her and gave her a pointed glance, but she needed to know.

Uncle Mitch narrowed his eyes. "I will be fog keeper for a long time, so no need to plan for that just yet."

"Totally," Tuck said, giving Sam a stop-asking-questions look.

She ignored him and held her uncle's intent gaze, still needing to know more. "What happened to Aunt Sylvie here?"

He frowned and crossed his arms, the old Uncle Mitch returning. "She disappeared."

"On the island?" Sam went on, unable to stop.

Uncle Mitch's frown deepened. Then his face sagged, and he uncrossed his arms. "She's gone and will never come back."

"Did it have something to do with the wondrous and terrible secret?"

He jerked his head up, wrinkling

his forehead, and stared across the flames at her with shiny eyes. "Yes. I wanted to protect you from it, so you didn't disappear, too…," he said, his words trailing off.

"I understand," Sam said.

Uncle Mitch slumped. "You do?"

"You were upset over losing Aunt Sylvie and didn't want to lose me. You showed it by getting mad, but you still wanted to protect me."

Uncle Mitch gave Sam a soft smile, and Tuck stopped nudging her.

"Were you really going to send me away?" Sam whispered.

"I didn't want to, but your mom entrusted me to keep you safe."

"You're not the worst uncle ever," she said.

"Maybe just the worst cook," he said, cocking his head with a smile.

"Me, too," Sam said.

Uncle Mitch's smile widened, but he crinkled his eyes as if something pained him. He hunched back down against the wall. Sam realized that they had more in common than she'd thought, and it wasn't just about burning food. *We've both been mostly alone for so long that it's hard to open up to people.*

The three of them sat in silence, watching over Barloc. The fire crumbled to red embers and then to ash.

Sam had one more question. "What happens if Barloc dies?"

Uncle Mitch sighed. "A bit of magic dies on the island, and that opens a window for darker dangers to rise."

She and Tuck shared a look. Again, with the darker dangers. "What does that mean?"

Uncle Mitch poked the fire as if seeking an answer in it, but he didn't respond.

"What if my mom came here to check on Barloc?" Tuck asked. "She can cure him, I know it."

"Absolutely not," said Uncle Mitch. "We can't risk one more person knowing about this island."

"Then what if we brought Barloc to her?" Tuck asked.

Sam nodded excitedly. "Good idea!"

"No," Uncle Mitch said in a flat tone. "We cannot take a magical creature from this island. He could die."

"He could die *here*," Sam said, raising her voice and throwing up her hands in frustration.

"We wait until dawn." Uncle Mitch's voice was stern.

The meadow grew quiet except for Verny's snores and the occasional snorts of the unicorns rolling around in their sleep. Sam's eyes kept closing, as did Tuck's.

"Go to sleep, you two," Uncle Mitch said. "I'll wake you before dawn, in a couple of hours."

Tuck finally gave in and fell asleep on his side. Sam was just about to drift off herself when Uncle Mitch spoke quietly. "Sam, promise me one thing."

She sat up straighter, shivering under her blanket. Uncle Mitch brought her another one from a chest in the hut's corner. She waited as he covered her with it, peering down with a solemn look on his face.

"If you ever return without me, promise me you'll never cross the mountain and go to the other side of the island. It's not safe."

"I promise," she said. Uncle Mitch started to stand up, but she took his hand. "I know what it's like to lose someone. I won't abandon you, like my dad abandoned me."

Uncle Mitch touched her hair.

"I know your heart, Sam." His voice cracked. "You'd never leave behind someone you love, would you?"

She shook her head, feeling an ache in her throat as he held her gaze. Then, to her surprise, he kissed the top of her head before melting into the shadows. She tried to keep her eyes open but quickly fell asleep to the sound of magical creatures breathing all around her.

It seemed like Sam had just closed her eyes when Uncle Mitch gently shook her and Tuck awake. His face loomed, tight and pinched, as a lantern swayed in his hand.

"Barloc is dying."

Sam and Tuck threw off their blankets, shivering in the cool air, and went to the baby unicorn. He was struggling harder for breath, his chest shuddering up and down. He coughed, and froth foamed at his mouth and nose. His coat was shiny with sweat.

"We've got to get him to my mom," Tuck said.

Uncle Mitch stood over them, hands clenched.

"Tuck's right," Sam said. "Let's go. It's his only chance."

Finally, Uncle Mitch nodded,

handed the lantern to Sam, and wrapped Barloc in a blanket. The unicorn whinnied, but didn't resist.

They stepped out into the meadow. The unicorn herd stood in a line before them, with Verny sitting in the middle, eyes glittering and tail snapping. The moon watched over them as the black sky faded to gray and the stars melted away.

"We'll bring him back, no matter what I must do," Uncle Mitch said to the herd.

Save one, save us all, their voices called in Sam's head.

I'll do my best. I promise, she thought.

We expect you will, Samantha Sea Wells.

Awed by the trust they had in her, she bowed to them. The unicorns parted for them and they took off at a canter through the meadow and into the woods, back toward the beach.

Verny flew overhead this time, his great wings shadowing them from above. Blue lightning bugs dashed about as if to help speed them along, and in the gentle breeze, the plants waved their leaves in unison. *Hurry, there's not much time,* their song seemed to say.

Sam, Tuck, and Uncle Mitch had nearly reached the beach when the

island swayed beneath their feet
and a great groan filled the air. Sam
and Tuck crashed into one another,
stumbling as the island rocked.

"An earthquake!" Tuck yelled.

"Worse," Uncle Mitch yelled back,
running faster. He clutched Barloc
to his chest, but another tremor sent
him tumbling headlong into a tree.
He slid to the ground and didn't
move, Barloc still in his arms.

"Uncle Mitch!" Sam and Tuck
held on to the trees for support as
they struggled to reach him. Once
Sam was by her uncle's side, her first
aid training kicked in. Mom had
made her take the class in case she
ever got hurt while home alone.

"Grab Barloc," she yelled to Tuck. Startled, he did as she said, pulling the baby unicorn from her uncle's limp arms. The ground shifted again. Sam grabbed a tree trunk to stop herself from falling sideways.

When the tremor passed, she knelt by Uncle Mitch and checked to see if he was breathing. "His chest is moving," she said, relieved. "Help me lay him flat, Tuck."

Tuck placed Barloc on the ground, and together they moved Uncle Mitch's slumped body so he was resting on his back.

The ground seized beneath them, knocking Sam and Tuck into each other.

"Wake up, Uncle Mitch. Oh, please wake up," Sam wished aloud, picking up Barloc and cradling him in her arms. He whimpered and then was quiet as the ground finally stilled.

Uncle Mitch coughed. He shuddered, then coughed again. He opened his eyes, focusing on Sam and then Tuck. "What happened?"

"You got knocked out," Sam said.

Her uncle sat up groggily and touched the back of his head. "It hurts, but I'll be all right," he said.

Sam's heart slowed, but then the earth began to pitch again.

"We've got to get off the island," Uncle Mitch said. He stood up

unsteadily and took off down the path. Tuck and Sam, holding Barloc, followed and burst out onto the beach. Waves rose and crashed on the shore. Tuck's boat was gone, a speck in the distance, carried out to sea.

Verny landed beside them and immediately fell on his side as the ground shook. He screeched, flapping his wings to get up and blowing out a big breath that froze a row of trees.

"We can't all fit in my boat. Fly home on Verny," Uncle Mitch urged, his eyes wild. He took Barloc from Sam. "Wind the fog clock, and get Mel to meet us at her clinic."

"Fly on a dragon?" Tuck gulped. "Isn't there another way?"

Verny roared out frosty clouds and tapped Tuck's head with his elbow, sending him flat on his butt in the sand.

"Wyvern," Sam corrected, helping him up. They clung to each other as the sand rocked at their feet. "Uncle Mitch is right. We've got no choice."

"Mom will kill me for losing the boat," Tuck moaned.

"I think she'll be more upset about you flying on a wyvern," Sam said. The groaning of the island grew louder, drowning out her words. Tuck nodded with wide eyes.

Uncle Mitch placed Barloc in his boat, then untied it. Sam hugged her uncle hard. He squeezed her back, then practically fell into the boat as the island shuddered. "Hurry, now. I'll meet you at the clinic," he said as Tuck and Sam pushed the boat into the sea.

Uncle Mitch rowed away, pumping his arms fast, waves slapping at the boat. Sam feared she'd never see him again.

Be strong. We need you, Barloc's voice spoke in her head.

I need you, too. And Sam realized how true it was. The unicorns had given her purpose.

Verny flattened his back and wings on the beach, offering the kids a ride. Sam took the first step and climbed on top of the wyvern. His scales were soft, and he smelled like salt and pine. Tuck swayed on the sand, his face pale in the fading moonlight.

Sam held out her hand. "Just like riding a horse."

He choked out an awkward laugh and took her hand, climbing up to sit in front of her.

They lifted off over the sea, the brisk tailwind helping them along, and soared toward home.

Tuck gasped every time he looked down. "Riding a wyvern is scary, but I'm even more worried about what your Uncle Mitch said. What could be worse than an earthquake on the island?"

"I have no idea," Sam said as she glanced at the choppy water far below her.

The sky grew lighter.

"Faster, Verny," Sam whispered.

"No, not faster!" Tuck called out, clinging to Verny's neck.

Verny cackled and sped up, shooting across the sea like an arrow. They zoomed over Uncle Mitch, his boat pressed against the dark waves below. He lifted his hand in greeting. They left him behind and soon landed on the beach in front of his house.

Tuck and Sam slid off.

"Goodbye, Verny. Thanks for everything."

The wyvern bowed, then bent his head, shaking his necklace.

"I think he wants you to have his unicorn necklace," Tuck said.

Verny nodded with a grin, tapping Tuck's shoulder with a wing.

Sam gently lifted the necklace off of Verny, clutching it in her hand. *I'm a unicorn protector now.* She hugged Verny. "I hope I get to see you again someday."

Verny sniffed with a tilt of his head, then smiled and lifted off, flying toward the rising sun and Unicorn Island.

"Come on, Tuck!" Sam slipped the necklace into her pocket, then ran up the stairs to Uncle Mitch's house, Tuck right beside her.

They quickly wound the fog clock back to full and headed toward Tuck's house.

"Now we have to tell my mom that unicorns are real," Tuck said as they ran down the street.

"She'll believe you," Sam said, breathing hard as she pushed her exhausted legs to move faster. "She'll have to, once she sees Barloc."

He nodded, glancing at the sea, and skidded to a stop. "Sam, look!"

The fog bank had slipped down over the island, hiding it once more.

The wondrous secret was safe for now, but they still had to save a baby unicorn.

CHAPTER

10

What's this emergency, Tucker?" his mom asked. She was drinking the coffee she'd made when they got to her office. "It must be serious for you to wake me up before dawn and drag me here."

"I can't tell you until Mr. Mardock

gets here," Tuck said, chewing on his bottom lip.

Sam jumped in, twisting her hands in front of her. "It's life or death, and you're the only one who can help us."

Mel raised her eyebrows. She tapped her fingers on the front counter. Headlights flashed across the window.

"He's here!" Sam said, rushing for the door. She and Tuck held it open as Uncle Mitch carried Barloc in, completely covered by the blanket except for his hoofs.

"Bring him into the back room," Mel said, thrusting open the door to her office.

Uncle Mitch gently placed the bundle on the steel table and lifted the blanket.

Mel gasped, her mouth hanging open. She stepped back into a cabinet, rattling the glass window. "Is that really what I think it is?"

She darted her gaze from Uncle Mitch to Barloc.

"Yes," Uncle Mitch said. "He was born two nights ago, much smaller than most, and within a few hours he became sick."

"He's dying, Mom," Tuck said.

Sam stroked Barloc's neck. He shivered beneath her fingers. "You're our only hope, Dr. Thompson."

With those words, Tuck's mom

snapped into action. "Tell me all of his symptoms," she said.

While Uncle Mitch listed them all, Mel inspected Barloc, talking to herself. "Similar to a horse, I see...there's swelling around the eyes and face...discharge from the nose and mouth...fever, coughing... difficulty breathing..."

Her hands lingered on his horn as she carefully examined his head and chest. He whimpered under her hands. "It's all right, sweet boy. We'll take care of you."

Barloc raised his head and shook his mane at her with a weak snort, gazing into her eyes. She froze. "Can you understand me?"

Barloc nodded, then rested his head on the table.

"His name is Barloc," Uncle Mitch said wearily. "He lives on the island with all the other unicorns that I care for."

Mel frowned. "What island?"

"There's a hidden island in the fog bank," Tuck told his mom.

"I see." Mel looked in Barloc's mouth and ears. "And you went there, Tucker?"

"Yes." He spoke barely above a whisper while looking at his feet.

"Only because I asked him to," Sam said. "He helped us save Barloc."

Tuck gave her a grateful look. His mom didn't need to know that he'd lost their boat *and* ridden on a sort-of dragon.

"Can you cure him?" Uncle Mitch asked.

Mel cleared her throat. She began to gather supplies from the cabinet. "He has something similar to African horse sickness, which is spread by insects and causes fever, plus heart and breathing problems. But there have been no known cases of it in the United States."

"Will he live?" Sam asked, leaning on Uncle Mitch. He put an arm around her, squeezing her shoulder.

Mel readied a syringe and injected it into Barloc's hip. "I'm treating him as I would a horse, giving him antibiotics and something for his cough and fever. He might even need oxygen." She didn't answer Sam's question.

"What's the survival rate for this African horse sickness?" Uncle Mitch asked.

Mel placed her hands on the table. "Five percent," she said quietly.

They were all silent at that.

Then Sam remembered Uncle Mitch's injury. "My uncle smashed into a tree and was knocked out," she told Mel. "Can you check him out, too?"

"I can do a few simple things." Mel inspected Uncle Mitch's head and asked him questions about the time and date and where he was. When he answered them all correctly, she nodded. "You probably don't have a concussion, but you should go to the hospital to be thoroughly checked out."

Uncle Mitch shook his head and gave a rare grin. "I'm fine."

Sam was glad that her uncle didn't seem to be seriously injured. "Can we stay and watch over Barloc?" she asked Mel.

Mel folded her hands and looked at them. Finally, she nodded. "Help me get him into a more comfortable, private examination room. I will set up two cots in the room so you can rest while you stay with him."

Together they lifted Barloc, now sound asleep, and carefully carried him to a back room. They arranged blankets on the ground there and laid him down on them. His pearly coat shone like a seashell and his horn glimmered in the fluorescent lighting.

"I have to open up the clinic," Mel said, looking at her watch. "I'll check on Barloc throughout the day, and I'll make sure no one comes in here."

"When will we know if...he's going to make it?" Sam asked.

"By this evening," Mel said with a tight smile. She opened the door and left, glancing back before softly shutting the door.

At Uncle Mitch's insistence, Tuck and Sam flopped onto the cots. Then Uncle Mitch stood over Barloc just as he'd stood over the unicorn family for years—and, Sam knew, would for years to come.

Mom had chosen Uncle Mitch to be Sam's protector, and now Sam chose him, too. She fell asleep feeling like she had finally found a place to call home.

Throughout the day, Mel popped in to check on Barloc. Sam and Tuck made sure the baby unicorn drank water and slurped the mash that Mel brought in. Uncle Mitch ran out to get them all sandwiches and drinks.

By 8 p.m., the clinic was closed, and the staff were on their way home. Mel came into the room to examine Barloc. They all gathered around.

"Fever's gone," she said excitedly, touching his face. "And the swelling's gone down, too." She listened to his chest. "His lungs are much clearer. What a fast recovery. I think he's going to make it!"

"He's got magic on his side," Sam said, giving Tuck a high five as Uncle Mitch staggered back and sat down with a huge sigh of relief. Barloc lifted his head and licked Mel's hand. She laughed, and he nudged her with his horn. Then, to everyone's surprise, he tossed his mane and pushed himself upright with shaky legs. He wobbled a bit before standing up strong, his violet eyes sparkling.

Sam fell to her knees and threw

her arms around his neck. "Beautiful Barloc, I'm so happy."

You make me happy, too, Samantha.

Uncle Mitch looked up and gave Sam a proud smile. They'd saved the unicorn—together.

"We need to take him back to the island right now," he said.

Mel put her hands on her hips and shook her head with a frown. "He needs to be monitored overnight and given more antibiotics."

Uncle Mitch stood and wrapped Barloc in his blanket. "He needs to go back to the island. The longer he's away, the more magic he loses." He picked up the baby unicorn. "We have no choice. Right, Barloc?"

Barloc nodded.

"Then let me come with you," Mel insisted. "If one unicorn is sick, the others could be, too."

She rushed about to gather supplies in a bag, but Uncle Mitch put a hand on her arm and shook his head. "No. Too many humans breaking through the fog can disrupt the magic that keeps these special creatures hidden. Sam, Tuck, and I will return Barloc right now. We can monitor the other unicorns for signs of sickness."

Mel looked from him to Sam and Tuck, then nodded slowly. She finished packing the bag of medical supplies and handed it to Uncle Mitch. "Instructions are on the medicine bottles."

"I'll do my best."

She fished in her pocket for her keys. "And take my motorboat."

"Thank you," Uncle Mitch said, pocketing the keys.

Sam covered up Barloc's horn where the blanket had slipped, and they headed toward the front door.

"Take care of them," Mel called, hugging Tuck tightly before letting go. "Take care of my son, too."

"I will," Uncle Mitch said. He shook Mel's hand, and then he, Sam, and Tuck left to take Barloc back to his herd.

They cruised through the sea toward the fog bank, a million gold sparkles on the water. When they got far enough away from shore, Barloc shed his blanket and stood at the front of the boat, swishing his tail and sniffing the salty breeze. He whinnied and pawed the air with glee, his horn gleaming in the sun's last rays like a silver sword.

No one spoke on the journey back. *Maybe their hearts are full, like mine,* Sam thought, unable to stop smiling.

The sun slipped beneath the horizon and the purple-orange sky dipped into black, stars popping out above. Uncle Mitch steered them into the fog bank, and the world they knew disappeared. Unicorn Island rose green and mysterious before them.

"I'm so glad you came to Foggy Harbor, Sam," Tuck said, breaking the silence.

Sam nodded her head. "Me, too." Suddenly, she giggled.

"What's so funny?"

"I never thought I'd say that," she said.

"Me either, gilly soose." Tuck made a face, and they both laughed.

Uncle Mitch turned on the boat's lights and eased them slowly toward shore. As they glided toward the beach, they heard the sound of metal scraping against sand. The boat lurched to a stop in the shallows.

Uncle Mitch switched off the motor and studied the water. He shook his head. "I should have realized it's not deep enough for this boat to get to shore. We'll have to let Barloc off here and return later, in my rowboat."

Sam knelt in front of Barloc and laid her hand on his pure white coat. *Can you get back to the herd by yourself?*

Barloc nodded at her. Tuck

saluted goodbye and Sam hugged the baby unicorn, inhaling his sweet scent of hay and saltwater.

Place your forehead on mine, he said.

She did, feeling his warm coat.

Now make a wish.

Sam closed her eyes, waves gently rocking the boat.

I wish to be a fog keeper and protect you always.

She pulled her head back and gave Barloc a parting pat on his side. Barloc leaped from the boat and swam to shore. No quakes jolted the island. All was peaceful.

With a glance back, Barloc kicked his hooves in the air and then raced

off through the woods. Verny flew out from beyond the trees. He dipped his wings at them and shot off back over the island.

Uncle Mitch steered them back to Foggy Harbor, its lights pulling them toward its quiet haven.

"What did you wish for, Sam?" Uncle Mitch asked.

Sam's eyes widened. "How did you know?"

"Know what?" Tuck asked, holding on to the edge of the boat.

"That unicorns can grant

wishes," Uncle Mitch said.

"What? They can?" Tuck sat up straight. "I wish I'd known that. I've got lots of wishes!" He sighed and collapsed back on the bench.

"Maybe next time," Uncle Mitch said. "And by the way, don't worry about the boat you lost. I'll build you a new one."

"Thanks!" Tuck brightened with that news.

Sam pulled out the photo of Aunt Sylvie and handed it to her uncle. "I'm sorry I took this. It's just that she looks like me, and…"

"And that makes you feel like you're connected to her, and me, and this place."

She nodded, swallowing hard.

"Maybe we can get our photo taken together," he said.

"Cool." She put a hand on the steering wheel. Uncle Mitch placed his hand over hers, and they navigated the water side by side.

One more thing bothered Sam. "Barloc told me I would see my real mom someday," she said. "What did he mean?"

"He was really sick," Uncle Mitch said quickly. "I'm sure he was just confused."

"The unicorns also said they were expecting me."

"Well, of course, because I told them about you."

Ah, that makes sense, she thought.

"And you can understand their thoughts," he went on.

She nodded and he sighed. Sam wasn't sure if it was a sigh of relief or fear, but she didn't want to ask. Everything actually seemed to be okay for once, and she didn't want to spoil the moment.

But there was still one more important thing to share. "I want to stay and take care of the unicorns with you," she announced. "That was my wish—to be a fog keeper in training."

Uncle Mitch looked straight ahead, his jaw twitching.

"It's not an easy job."

"I know," she said. "But I also know that I can do it."

He finally peered down at her, considering her words. "I see that Verny gave you his unicorn necklace."

Sam nodded, gripping the necklace and holding Uncle Mitch's stare.

He cleared his throat. "You did prove yourself today, helping me—and saving me, too."

"And I'm more than ready to face what lies ahead if it means I can care for these wild, beautiful, magical animals," Sam said. She paused, gathering her courage. "Maybe even after my mom comes back from her tour I can stay with you and spend the rest of the summer here."

Tuck's mouth fell open and then he grinned his biggest grin ever, moving to her side as they neared Foggy Harbor. He raised his eyebrows at her as they both waited for her uncle to say something.

Uncle Mitch took her hand and held it tight, then nodded as they reached the harbor, the lights of the town leading them in.

They were home.

The herd rejoiced over the baby unicorn's return, racing around the meadow, but Truad sensed that something was different. As Barloc's adoptive mother, she was more in tune with him than any other member of the herd was. Only she knew that Barloc's magic light had dimmed, as if the real world had sucked it from him.

That night, the herd slept a deep sleep, at peace because they knew all was as it should be, but Truad awoke, disturbed by a nightmare.

Drawn to the top of the mountain, she bolted there and peered over to the other side of the island. Below her on the slope, the mountain ridges cracked and buckled as if a great giant lived beneath them and sought escape. Sand shifted on the beach

below, two fists forming and then sinking away.

Then all was still.

Darker dangers were coming.

Epilogue

Mel sat in her office, thinking and waiting for Tuck to return. The wall clock ticked to the rhythm of her heart. Her mind tumbled with thoughts about everything that had happened that day.

Unicorns. Here in Foggy Harbor.

She flicked on her desk lamp, grabbed a notebook, and began to write furiously.

I, Melanie Thompson, doctor of veterinarian medicine, am the first person in the medical community to encounter a real unicorn, treat it for illness, and cure it. Through me, the world will come to know and understand these magical creatures. No longer are they fantastical beasts from fairytales. And, finally, I can prove it.

She paused, chewing on her pen, then continued writing late into the night.

THE HISTORY OF UNICORNS

People have been sharing tales about unicorns since ancient times. They're usually described as wild creatures with magical powers that are nearly impossible to capture.

Some used to believe those who drank from a unicorn horn would be protected from illness. In medieval times, narwhal tusks and rhinoceros horns were sometimes sold as and mistaken for mythical unicorn horns, and people made cups out of them to drink from.

Artists throughout history have depicted unicorns in paintings, engravings, tapestries, and other works. Today, unicorns often appear in stories as symbols of good luck and purity. Unicorns are particularly beloved in Scotland, where they are the country's national animal!

ALL ABOUT WYVERNS

As Sam and Tuck discover, unicorns aren't the only living things on the island. It is also home to Verny, a friendly wyvern who helps the kids and even protects the unicorns, too.

Wyverns are mythical creatures who have appeared in stories for hundreds of years. The main difference between wyverns and dragons is that wyverns have only two legs, but, like Verny, they're also often smaller and don't breathe fire.

Today, wyverns appear in books, movies, and video games, and sometimes they pop up on flags and crests and as mascots for sports teams.

The word "wyvern" comes from the Latin word that means "viper." From his soft scales to his long tail, Verny slightly resembles a snake— but one that's kind, not poisonous, and *very* protective of his friends.

WHAT DOES A VETERINARIAN DO?

Tuck's mom, Dr. Melanie Thompson, is an important person in Foggy Harbor. As the town veterinarian, she treats cats, dogs, and more.

After earning a college degree, a veterinarian must study for several years at a veterinary school. Some vets specialize in common household pets, while others focus on farm or zoo animals, wildlife, or horses. Their jobs can include treating diseases, performing surgery, and providing dental care, but they also spend a lot of time preventing sickness, just like your doctor does at a yearly checkup.

Some veterinarians conduct important research to help find cures for ailments, identify new problems, or share surprising discoveries in medical publications.

PIRATES OF THE CAROLINAS

Before Sam leaves for Foggy Harbor, her mother tells her the Carolina coast was famous for shipwrecks and pirate stories. Indeed, North and South Carolina were visited by many pirates, including perhaps the most famous of them all: Blackbeard.

Born Edward Teach, Blackbeard spent a lot of time capturing and stealing from ships in the early port cities of Bath, North Carolina, and Charleston, South Carolina.

In 1718, Blackbeard's ship, the Queen Anne's Revenge, ran aground and sank off the North Carolina coast. The wreckage was discovered more than 250 years later. Today, visitors can see artifacts from the ship and take pirate-themed tours to learn more about the area's fascinating history.

ISLANDS OF WILD HORSES

After Sam discovers Unicorn Island, her life is forever changed. And while there may not be any *real* unicorn islands in America, there are a few places where visitors can see some creatures that are pretty magical.

Ocracoke Island in North Carolina is known for its wild horses, which may date all the way back to the 17th century. Legend has it that the horses survived when European ships carrying livestock crashed on the rocky shores. Today, they're cared for by the National Park Service, and thousands of visitors come to see them each year.

In Maryland and Virginia, Assateague Island is home to a special breed of horse called the Chincoteague pony. These ponies are also featured in Marguerite Henry's popular children's book, *Misty of Chincoteague.*

ABOUT THE AUTHOR

DONNA GALANTI wanted to be a writer ever since she wrote a screenplay at seven years old and acted it out with the neighborhood kids. She attended an English school, housed in a magical castle, where her wild imagination was held back only by her itchy uniform (bowler hat and tie included!). She now lives with her family and two crazy cats in an old farmhouse and is the author of the middle-grade fantasy adventures *Joshua and the Lightning Road* and *Joshua and the Arrow Realm*.

ABOUT THE ILLUSTRATOR

BETHANY STANCLIFFE is a central Washington–based artist who grew up in the Rockies, where she spent her time building tree forts, reading fairy tales, and filling up sketchbooks. Following in the footsteps of her parents, Bethany studied art and illustration at BYU-Idaho. She draws her inspiration from nature, films, and childhood adventures. When she's not painting, she enjoys exploring outside with her son, Max, and creating original stories with her husband.